To my mother.

To my friend Mari. —E.M.

All rights reserved. Published by Orchard Books, an imprint of Scholastic Inc., *Publishers since 1920.* ORCHARD BOOKS and design are registered trademarks of Watts Publishing Group, Ltd., used under license. SCHOLASTIC and associated logos are trademarks and/or registered trademarks of Scholastic Inc.

The publisher does not have any control over and does not assume any responsibility for author or third-party websites or their content.

Library of Congress Cataloging-in-Publication Data available

ISBN 978-1-338-64821-8

10 9 8 7 6 5 4 3 2 1   21 22 23 24 25

Printed in Malaysia 108
First edition, January 2021

Book design by Rae Crawford

The text type was set in Mrs. Ant Regular.
The illustrations were created using collage, digital scanning, and Photoshop.

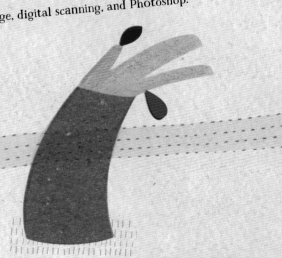

FINDING HOME

Estelí Meza

ORCHARD BOOKS
An Imprint of
Scholastic Inc.
New York

With the arrival of fall came a gust of
wind that blew Conejo's house away.

Conejo followed the trace of the wind until he felt very tired. He began to wonder if he would ever find his house, when all of a sudden, he heard Lobo Lobito honking his horn.

"Hi, Conejo! Do you want to go for a ride?"
"I'm in luck!" said Conejo. "Will you help me
look for my house?"

Together, they drove over mountains
and crossed valleys.
But they didn't find Conejo's house.

Lobo Lobito tried to cheer him up.
"Everything will be all right.
Say cheese, Conejo!"

Conejo set off again in a good mood.
"Bye, Lobo Lobito. Thank you!"

Conejo walked and walked until
he came to a colorful jungle.
The branches shook in a nearby tree.
It was his friend Perezoso.
"You look worried, Conejo."
"I'm searching for my house.
A gust of wind carried it away."
"Let's look for it together!" said Perezoso.

They climbed the tallest tree in the jungle
and looked out over a sea of leaves.
"I don't see your house, Conejo. I'm sorry."

"But I have something for you!
A little gift. My very favorite flower."
"I love it!" said Conejo. "See you soon, Perezoso.
Thanks for everything."
Conejo set off, feeling hopeful.

After leaving the jungle behind,
Conejo traveled to a small town.
"Hi, Buhíta," he called. "Can I come in?"
"Of course, Conejo. You are always welcome here."

Conejo told Buhíta about his troubles over a cup of hot tea.

"You know, Conejo? Maybe I can't help you find
your house, but I'll give you my music
and my stories."

Conejo set off once more,
filled with warmth.

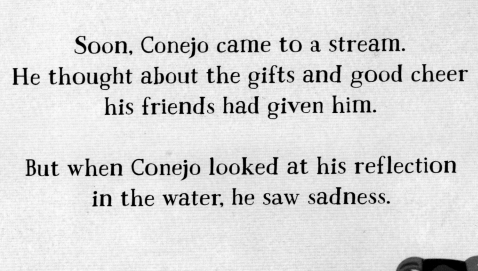

Soon, Conejo came to a stream.
He thought about the gifts and good cheer
his friends had given him.

But when Conejo looked at his reflection
in the water, he saw sadness.

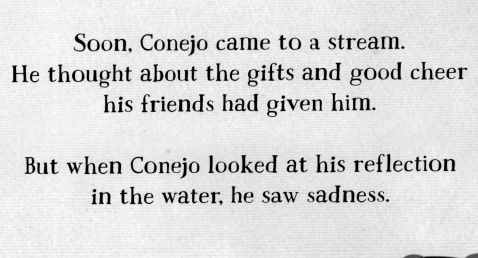

Soon, Conejo came to a stream.
He thought about the gifts and good cheer
his friends had given him.

But when Conejo looked at his reflection
in the water, he saw sadness.

Conejo sat with sadness
for some time.

When the rain had cleared,
Conejo felt a breeze that blew
in a different direction than before.

Conejo

Conejo did not find his old house.
But he found his way.
He filled his new home
with memories.
A photo. A flower. A book.
And plenty of music and stories.

AUTHOR'S NOTE

My inspiration to create this book about losing a home and rebuilding came from personal experiences. In the fall of 2017, Puerto Rico was struck by Hurricane Maria, and around the same time Mexico City, where I live, was hit by a strong earthquake. So many were left homeless and had to rebuild from scratch.

It made me think about how the feeling of longing for home is universal. It is part of the immigrant experience. Those who leave their home countries behind and migrate elsewhere know this well. But even someone relocating to a new city or going to a new school can understand the journey of making a new home.

This is also a story about finding ourselves. Sometimes things get complicated all of a sudden, and it can be difficult to see our path forward. It is important to sit with our complicated feelings and explore them. And it is okay to turn to friends and loved ones when we need help. Sometimes sadness decides to stay with us for a moment, but this doesn't mean it will be forever. You are loved and you are strong, and when you are ready, you will find your way.

—Estelí Meza